THE LUMBERJACK'S BEARD

DUNCAN BEEDIE

Big Jim Hickory was a lumberjack.
He lived by a forest in a little log cabin.

He had big, burly shoulders
and an even bigger bristly beard.

Every day, he got up and
did his limbering-up exercises.

(It's very important to limber up
if you're a lumberjack.)

After a hearty breakfast of pancakes and maple syrup,
Jim slung his big, trusty axe over his big,
burly shoulder and headed out into the forest.

CHOP-CHOPPETY-CHOP went Jim's axe,

echoing through the valley as he felled tree after tree after tree.

After a long day of swinging, whacking, cleaving and hacking,

Jim headed back to his cabin.

That evening, when he was just about to go to bed,
he heard a **PECK-PECKITY-PECK** at the door.

Jim looked down to see a small and very cross bird. "I built a lovely
new nest in my tree," shrieked the bird, "and you chopped it down!"

Jim scratched his big, bristly chin. Then he had an idea.

"I suppose you could move into my beard," he said.

"Very well then!" said the bird and in she flew.

The next morning, Jim woke up earlier than normal due to
the bird chirping away at the crack of dawn.

He did his limbering-up exercises, got dressed and ate his breakfast
(with a little help from the new tenant in his beard).

Jim's next job was to strip all the branches and leaves
from the tree trunks and burn them on a big bonfire.

After a long day of chopping, snapping, burning and crackling,
Jim trudged back to his cabin for a well-earned rest.

No sooner had he laid down his axe
than he heard a noise at the door.
SCRATCH-SCRATCHETY-SCRATCH
He looked down to see a very
fed-up looking porcupine.

"Oi!" snapped the porcupine,
"I needed those leaves and pine
needles to make a nice, cosy shelter.
Where am I going to live now?"

Jim thought and scratched his big, bristly chin.
"Well," he said, "I suppose you could move into my beard too."
He bent down and the porcupine crawled in.

The next morning, Jim woke even earlier and attempted to do his limbering-up exercises. He looked in the mirror and scratched his big, bristly chin.

YOOOOOWWWW! He got porcupine quills in his fingers.

He tried to eat his breakfast . . .

. . . but lost his appetite when he noticed bird poo on his shirt.

Jim's job that day was to float all the
tree trunks down the river to the lumber yard.
One by one, he rolled the logs into
the fast-flowing water.

After a hard day of lugging, splashing,
rolling and crashing . . .

Jim staggered back to his cabin.
THWUMP-THWUMPETY-THWUMP went his door.
He looked down to see a very angry beaver on his doorstep.

"I spent all day building my nice new dam, and it got
smashed to bits by those logs you threw in the river!" he snarled.
Without a word, Jim picked up the beaver and put him in his beard.

Between the bird's chirping, the porcupine's prickling and
the beaver's thwumping, Jim didn't get much sleep that night.

He was too tired to do his limbering-up exercises in the morning and
the beaver's thwumping tail knocked his pancakes all over the floor.

"That's it!" cried Jim, "I can't take it any more!
You'll all have to move out today!"

"BUT WHERE WILL WE LIVE?"
gasped his friends.

As Jim scratched his big, bristly chin, he had a bold but brilliant idea.
He went into his bathroom, took out his trusty razor
and began to shave off his big, bristly beard.

Then he piled it up on his porch and the bird, the porcupine
and the beaver all moved into their new, cosy den.

That night, Jim slept better than he had done for some time.

He woke up and did some particularly vigorous limbering-up exercises and put on a fresh plaid shirt.

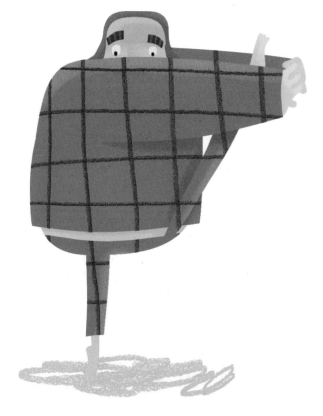

Then he made an enormous tower of pancakes and maple syrup.

After breakfast, Jim looked out of
the window at the bare ground where
the forest used to be and scratched his
unusually bare, stubbly chin.

And he had another brilliant idea . . .

That morning, Jim took his trusty shovel
and dug hole after hole after hole . . .

. . . and with his big hands,
he planted tree after tree after tree.

Jim's beard grew back over time.

The trees took quite a bit longer . . .

But it was worth the wait.

THE END

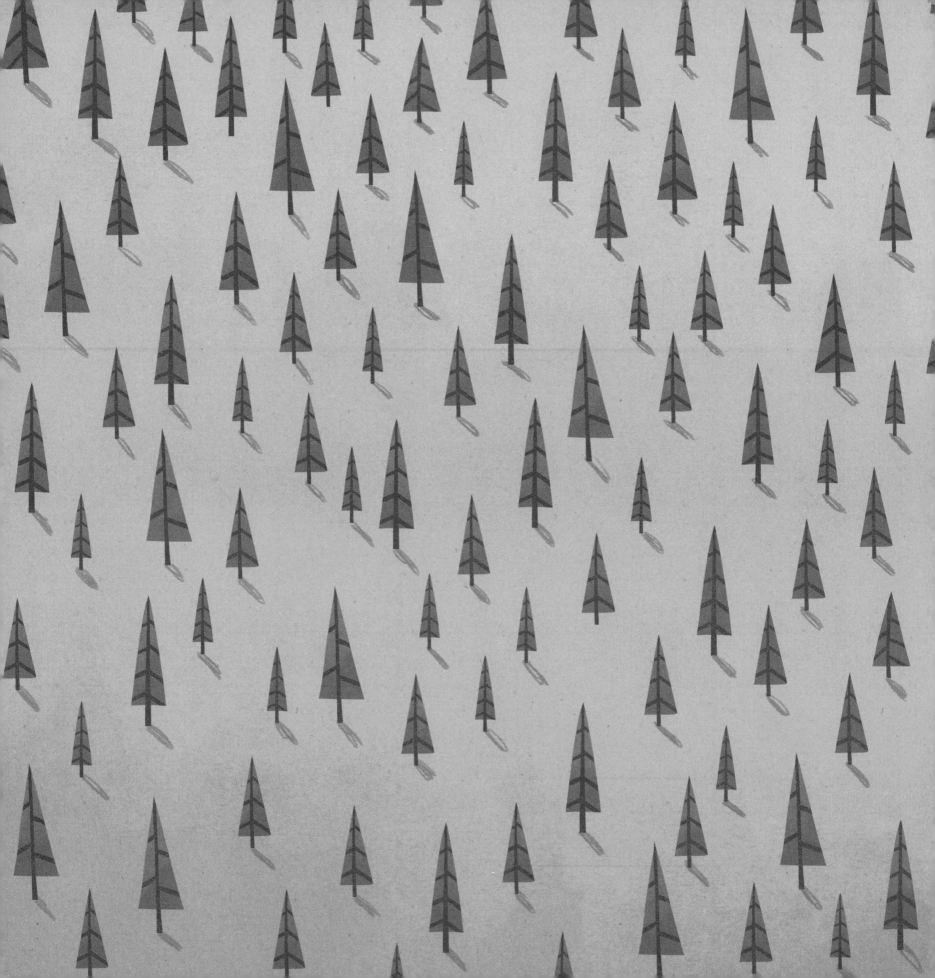